This
Harry
book belongs to

....

PUFFIN BOOKS

Published by the Penguin Group
Penguin Books Ltd, 80 Strand, London WC2R 0RL, England
Penguin Group (USA), Inc., 375 Hudson Street, New York, New York 10014, USA
Penguin Books Australia Ltd, 250 Camberwell Road, Camberwell, Victoria 3124, Australia
Penguin Books Canada Ltd, 10 Alcorn Avenue, Toronto, Ontario, Canada M4V 3B2
Penguin Books India (P) Ltd, 11 Community Centre, Panchsheel Park, New Delhi – 110 017, India
Penguin Group (NZ) Ltd, cnr Airborne and Rosedale Roads, Albany, Auckland 1310, New Zealand
Penguin Books (South Africa) (Pty) Ltd, 24 Sturdee Avenue, Rosebank 2196, South Africa

Penguin Books Ltd, Registered Offices: 80 Strand, London WC2R 0RL, England

www.penguin.com

First published in hardback by Gullane Children's Books 2002
First published in Puffin Books 2004
5 7 9 10 8 6

Text copyright © Ian Whybrow, 2002
Illustrations copyright © Adrian Reynolds, 2002
All rights reserved

The moral right of the author and illustrator has been asserted

Printed in China by Hung Hing

British Library Cataloguing in Publication Data
A CIP catalogue record for this book is available from the British Library

ISBN-13: 978-0-14056-983-4
ISBN-10: 0-14056-983-9

Harry and the Dinosaurs play Hide-and-Seek

Ian Whybrow and Adrian Reynolds

PUFFIN

Harry and
the dinosaurs are
playing hide-and-seek!

Can you help Harry
to find his dinosaurs?

Who's that hiding under the blue cushion?

blue

blue

yellow

red

purple

green

Found you, Apatosaurus!

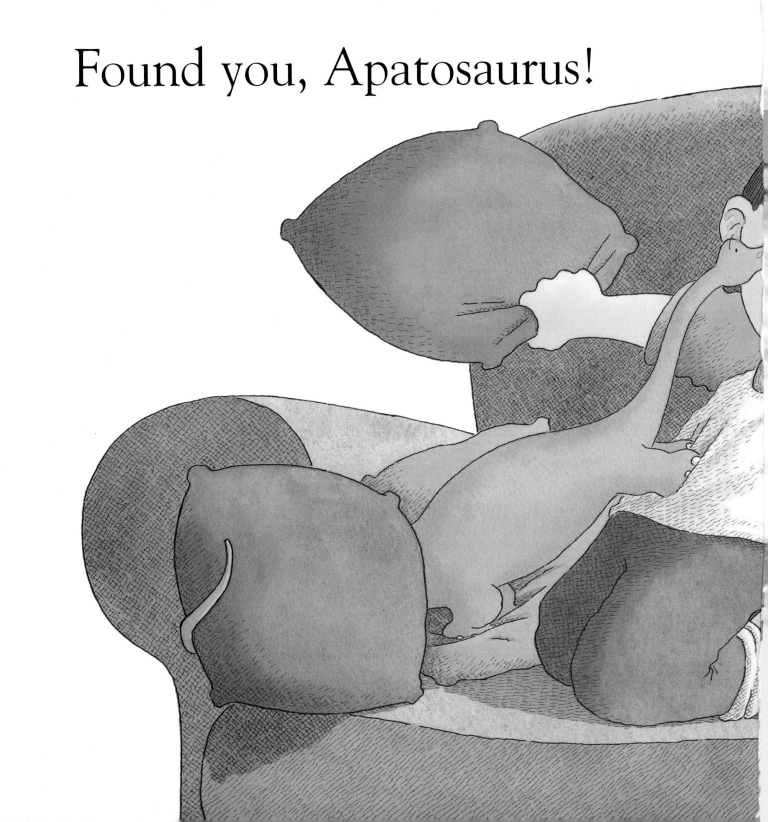

Who's that hiding under Harry's yellow hat?

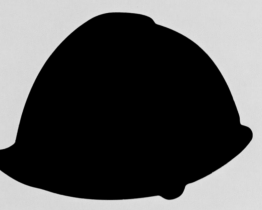

yellow

blue

yellow

red

purple

green

Found you, Triceratops!

Who's that
hiding behind
the red towel?

red

Found you, Tyrannosaurus!

Who's that hiding inside Nan's purple knitting basket?

purple

blue

yellow

red

purple

green

Found you, Stegosaurus!
And you, Anchisaurus!

Who's that
hiding inside
Mum's green boot?

green

blue

yellow

red

purple

green

Found you,
Scelidosaurus!

But now
where has
Harry gone?

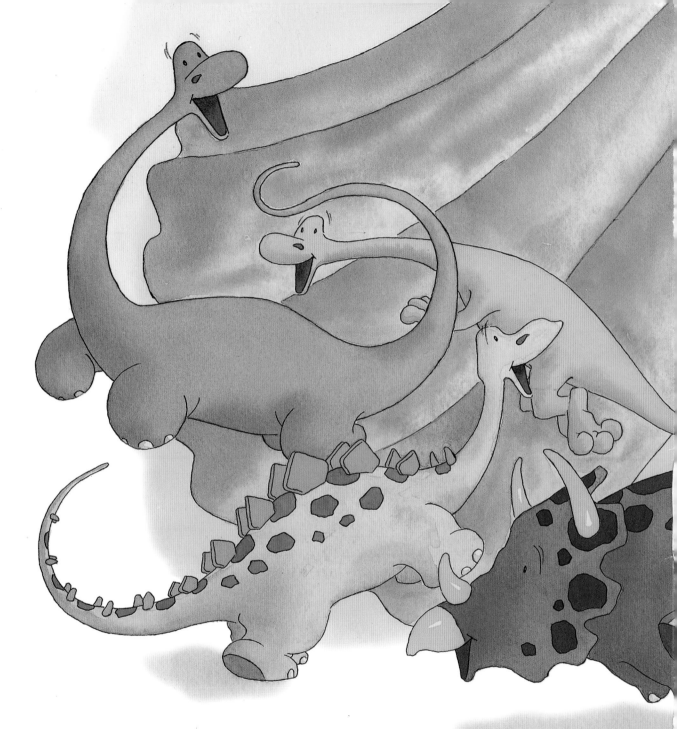

'Boo! Here I am!' says Harry.

Look out for all of Harry's adventures!

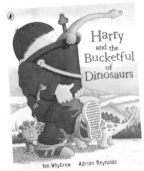

Harry and the Bucketful of Dinosaurs
Harry finds some old plastic dinosaurs and cleans them, finds out their names and takes them everywhere with him – until, one day, they get lost … Will he ever find them?

ISBN 0140569804

Harry and the Snow King
There's just enough snow for Harry to build a very small snow king. But then the snow king disappears – who's kidnapped him?

ISBN 0140569863

Harry and the Robots
Harry's robot is sent to the toy hospital to be fixed, so Harry and Nan decide to make a new one. When Nan has to go to hospital, Harry knows just how to help her get better!

ISBN 0140569820

Harry and the Dinosaurs say "Raahh!"
Harry's dinosaurs are acting strangely. They're hiding all over the house, refusing to come out … Could it be because today is the day of Harry's dentist appointment?

ISBN 0140569812

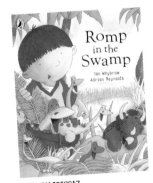

Harry and the Dinosaurs Romp in the Swamp
Harry has to play at Charlie's house and doesn't want to share his dinosaurs. But when Charlie builds a fantastic swamp, Harry and the dinosaurs can't help but join in the fun!

ISBN 0140569847

Harry and the Dinosaurs make a Christmas Wish
Harry and the dinosaurs would *love* to own a duckling. They wait till Christmas and make a special wish, but Santa leaves them something even more exciting…!

ISBN 0141380179 (hbk)
ISBN 0140569529 (pbk)